My Weirde[r School]

Mrs. Meyer Is on Fire!

Dan Gutman

Pictures by
Jim Paillot

HARPER

An Imprint of HarperCollinsPublishers

To Emma

My Weirdest School #4: Mrs. Meyer Is on Fire!

Text copyright © 2016 by Dan Gutman

Illustrations copyright © 2016 by Jim Paillot

Library of Congress Control Number: 2015947625

ISBN 978-0-06-228430-3 (trade bdg.)

ISBN 978-0-06-228432-7 (lib. bdg.)

Typography by Aurora Parlagreco

16 17 18 19 20   OPM   10 9 8 7 6 5 4 3 2 1

❖

First Edition

Contents

Super Vision

My name is A.J. and I hate birthdays.

Well, I don't hate *my* birthday. I like *my* birthday. But I don't like it when it's some-body else's birthday, because they get all the presents. They get all the attention. They get the first piece of cake. It's not fair!

Monday was crybaby Emily's birthday,

so we had to spend the whole morning in Mr. Cooper's class being nice to her.

"I'm so excited to go to your birthday party this weekend, Emily," said Andrea Young, this annoying girl with curly brown hair.

"Me too!" said Emily, who always agrees with everything Andrea says.

Ugh, disgusting! The guys and me were just happy that Emily didn't invite *us* to her birthday party. It is sure to be a real snoozefest.

After lunch the most amazing thing in the history of the world happened. Mr. Cooper came running into the class.

Well, that's not the amazing part. Mr.

Cooper comes running into the class all the time. The amazing part was that he came running into the class carrying a big pizza box!

"Whoa!" Mr. Cooper shouted as he tripped over the garbage can and almost slammed into the whiteboard.

Mr. Cooper is the only grown-up I know who wears a cape. He told us that he's a superhero from the East Pole.

I've heard of the North Pole. I've heard of the South Pole. But I've never heard of the East Pole. I think Mr. Cooper may have been yanking our chain.

"Don't worry!" he shouted as he put the pizza box on his desk. "Everything's fine. You're under my supervision."

"You have super vision?" I asked. "That is cool!"

"Did you use your super vision to heat up the pizza?" asked my friend Michael, who never ties his shoes.

"It's not a pizza," said Mr. Cooper as he

opened up the box. "It's a cake!"

Cake? I *love* cake! Cake is the *best*. There's nothing better than cake.*

"It's my birthday cake!" said Emily, clapping her hands together like it was her birthday or something.

Oh, wait a minute. It *was* her birthday.

"Emily's mom brought the cake to the front office," Mr. Cooper told us. "She made it with her own hands."

Big deal. It would be a lot harder to make a cake with somebody else's hands.

"Can I have the first piece?" asked my friend Ryan, who will eat anything, even

---

*Well, maybe cupcakes are better. I love them, too. But they're just little cakes that happen to be in cups, so it's the same stuff.

5

stuff that isn't food.

"Emily gets the first piece, of course," said Mr. Cooper. "She's the birthday girl."

We all gathered around Mr. Cooper's desk. He stuck nine candles into the cake and lit them. Then the whole class sang "Happy Birthday."

"Make a wish, Emily," said Andrea.

Emily closed her eyes. She was probably wishing for some girly-girl thing, like a Barbie doll, instead of something useful, like a football. Then she blew out the candles.

Or she *tried* to blow out the candles anyway. Emily was only able to blow out a few of them. So I decided to help her by blowing out the rest of the candles. And you'll never believe what happened next.

I'm not exactly sure what went wrong. Maybe I blew too hard or something. But the next thing we knew, one of the candles fell off the cake and landed on Emily's shirt!

"My shirt is on fire!" shouted Emily.

"Call the fire department!" shouted Alexia, this girl who rides a skateboard all the time.

"Run for your lives!" shouted Neil, who we call the nude kid even though he wears clothes.

Emily was on the floor, freaking out.

"Have no fear," said Mr. Cooper. "This is

a job for Cooperman!"

I thought Mr. Cooper was going to use his superpowers to put out the fire. Like, maybe he could use his super vision to shoot microwave-freezing rays out of his eyes or something. That would be cool.

But Mr. Cooper didn't do anything like that. He ran over to the door and grabbed the fire extinguisher off the wall.

"Stand clear!" he shouted.

Mr. Cooper aimed the fire extinguisher at Emily and pulled the trigger. This white, foamy stuff shot all over her shirt. Then he sprayed the stuff all over the cake. That foamy goop was everywhere.

Fire extinguishers are cool. It would be

fun to have a fire extinguisher war.

"Hooray for Mr. Cooper!" shouted Michael. "He put out the fire! He's my hero! He's a *super*hero!"

You'd think Emily would have been grateful that I helped her blow out the candles. You'd think she would be happy that she wasn't on fire anymore. But it was just the opposite.

"My shirt is ruined! It's all your fault, A.J.!" she shouted. "And my cake is ruined, too!"

"Your cake isn't ruined," I told her. "It just has more frosting on it now."

I was just kidding about the frosting. Fire extinguisher goop probably tastes yucky. But Emily started crying, of course.

"This is my worst birthday *ever*!" she shouted as she ran out of the room.

Sheesh, get a grip! What a crybaby. All she did was catch on fire a little.

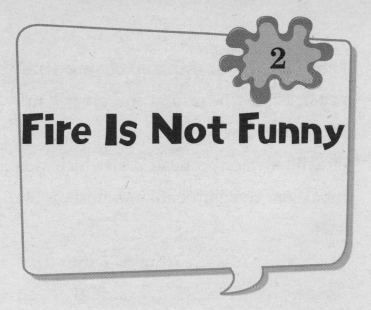

Fire Is Not Funny

It was a bummer that we couldn't eat Emily's birthday cake. But something even *worse* happened the next morning. We had an assembly. Ugh. Assemblies are boring.

Our principal, Mr. Klutz, was up on the stage. He has no hair at all. I mean *none*.

If you closed your eyes and put one hand on Mr. Klutz's head and the other hand on a honeydew, you'd never be able to tell which was the head and which was the melon. You'd probably want to eat his head.

Mr. Klutz was wearing a T-shirt that said RIOT on the front. On the back it said READING IS OUR THING.

Everybody was chitchatting as usual, so Mr. Klutz

made a peace sign, which means "shut up." We all stopped talking.

"There was a little incident in one of our classrooms yesterday," he announced. "It was a fire. Mr. Cooper was able to put it out, but if he hadn't acted quickly, the fire could have gotten out of control. Can you imagine if our school had burned down?"

In my head I imagined the school burning down. I imagined fire trucks in the street. I imagined flames and smoke everywhere. I imagined kids and teachers jumping out the windows. I imagined them landing on trampolines and bouncing back up to the windows.

Trampolines are cool. They should have

trampolines in our class instead of desks. Or maybe the whole floor could be one big trampoline.

Imagining weird stuff is fun. I went back to imagining that the school was burning down.

"No more school!" I shouted, jumping up from my seat. "No more school! No more school!"

I figured everybody was going to jump up from their seats and start chanting "No more school!" with me.

I looked around. Nobody else was standing. Nobody else was chanting. Everybody was looking at me.

I hate when that happens. I sat back

down in my seat. It was embarrassing. I wanted to go to Antarctica and live with the penguins.

"Because of the fire," said Mr. Klutz, "I invited a firefighter from the local fire station to come and talk to us about fire safety."

"Ooooh," we all went, because firefighters are cool.

Suddenly, lights started flashing. Sirens started screaming. A lady came out from behind the curtain. She was wearing a bright yellow raincoat and a red fire hat. She was holding an ax in her hand.

Axes are cool, but I don't know why she was carrying one. Hitting a fire with an

ax wouldn't be a good way to put it out, if
you ask me. You should spray water on a
fire or throw dirt on it.

One time my family went on a camping
trip, and my dad said I could pee on our

campfire to put it out. That was cool. Peeing on fires is fun.*

Anyway, you'll never guess in a million hundred years what the lady's name was, and I'm never going to tell you, and nothing you do will make me tell you.

I bet you're on pins and needles.

If you're on pins and needles, you should get off them and go sit on a chair or a couch or something. Sitting on pins and needles must hurt.

Okay, okay, I'll tell you. It was Mrs. Meyer!

"Let's give a nice round of applause for Mrs. Meyer," said Mr. Klutz. We all clapped

*Don't try this at home, kids. I'm a professional.

our hands in circles.

"Thank you," said Mrs. Meyer. "It will be easy to remember my name because 'Meyer' rhymes with 'fire.'"*

"That's funny," said Mr. Klutz.

"Oh, there's nothing funny about fire," said Mrs. Meyer, "but when I visit schools, I always like to start off with a joke. Why did the fireman wear red suspenders?"

"Why?" we all shouted.

"To hold his pants up!" said Mrs. Meyer.

Mr. Klutz and Mrs. Meyer started laughing even though she didn't say anything funny.

---

*Also, it will be easy to remember her name because it's right there on the book cover. But I guess she didn't know that.

I didn't get her joke. Suspenders? What are suspenders? If you want to hold your pants up, why not just wear a belt like a normal person? And if the fireman's pants keep falling down all the time, maybe he should get smaller pants. Or he should get a new job that doesn't involve so much running around. And why are the suspenders red anyhow? They could have been any color. I was confused.

If you ask me, that joke wasn't funny at all.

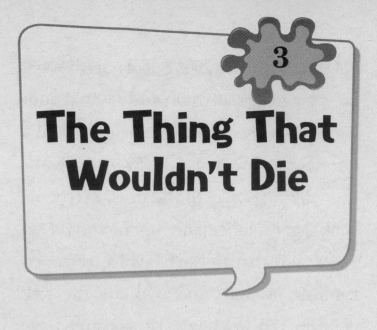

The Thing That Wouldn't Die

Mrs. Meyer was pacing back and forth across the stage as she talked to us.

"I know kids are curious about fire," she said, "and fire can be a wonderful thing. We use it to cook our food. We use it to warm our houses in the winter. But fire can be a *dangerous* thing, too. Did you kids know that every year in the United States, more than half a million houses burn down?"

"WOW," we all said, which is "MOM" upside down.

Mrs. Meyer told us that we should never play with matches, lighters, or fireworks. We should never touch radiators or heaters. We should never stick anything into an electrical socket. We should never put a blanket or a piece of clothing over a lamp.

She sure knew a lot of interesting stuff about fire. While she was talking, we were all glued to our seats.

Well, not really. That would be weird. You'd have to be crazy to glue yourself to a seat. How would you get the glue off your pants?

Anyway, Mrs. Meyer told us lots of other stuff we could do to prevent fires.

"Play with toys, kids," she said. "Not fire."

When she was finished talking, we walked a million hundred miles back to our classroom. Andrea was the line leader. Neil was the door holder.

"Okay," Mr. Cooper said after we had settled into our seats, "turn to page twenty-three in your math—"

He didn't get the chance to finish his sentence, because out in the hallway all these lights started flashing and sirens started screaming. And you'll never believe who walked into the door at that moment.

Nobody! It would hurt if you walked into a door. But you'll never believe who walked into the door*way*.

It was Mrs. Meyer!*

"To what do we owe the pleasure of your company, Mrs. Meyer?" asked Mr. Cooper.

(That's grown-up talk for "What are *you* doing here?")

"I'm going from class to class to check all the fire extinguishers and smoke detectors," said Mrs. Meyer.

Mr. Cooper closed his math book.

---

*Well, of *course* it was Mrs. Meyer. Who else could it be? It's a book about Mrs. Meyer!

"Go ahead," he said, but he didn't sound all that happy about it.

"First, I'd like to tell a joke," said Mrs. Meyer.

Another joke? I was still trying to figure out her *first* joke.

"What kind of crackers do firefighters put in their soup?" she asked us.

"I don't know," said Michael.

"I don't know," said Alexia.

"I don't know," said Ryan.

In case you were wondering, everybody was saying they didn't know.

"Firecrackers!" said Mrs. Meyer.

Everybody laughed even though she didn't say anything funny again. Mrs. Meyer took the fire extinguisher off the wall and looked at it. We already knew it worked, because Mr. Cooper had used it the day before to put out Emily.

Then Mrs. Meyer climbed up on a chair and carefully unscrewed the smoke detector from the ceiling.

"Smoke detectors save lives," she told us. "Your parents should have one on every floor of your house."

"If there was a smoke detector on every floor of our house," I said, "we would be tripping over smoke detectors all the time."

Everybody laughed even though I didn't say anything funny. Andrea rolled her eyes.

"Mrs. Meyer means the smoke detectors should be on the *ceilings*, Arlo!" she said.

That made no sense at all. If she meant

we should have smoke detectors on the ceilings, why did she say we should have them on the floors? Floors and ceilings are opposites.

"If you hear your smoke detector start beeping, get low and get out of your house," said Mrs. Meyer. "Repeat after me. Get low and go!"

"Get low and go!" we all chanted. "Get low and go!"

"Very good," Mrs. Meyer said. "Any questions about smoke detectors?"

Andrea started waving her hand around like she was trying to signal a plane. What a brownnoser.

Andrea *always* asks questions. She

thinks it makes you look smart when you ask questions. If you ask me, it's the other way around. If you know a lot of stuff, you don't need to ask questions. You only need to ask a lot of questions if you're a dumbhead like Andrea who doesn't know anything.

Mrs. Meyer called on her, of course.

"How does the smoke detector know there's smoke?" Andrea asked.

"Yeah," said Michael. "How can it smell if it doesn't have a nose?"

I imagined a smoke detector that was made in the shape of a nose. That would be cool. They should definitely sell them in stores.

"Good question," Mrs. Meyer replied.

"Smoke detectors don't need a nose. They have a light sensor in them that can see the smoke. Watch this."

She took a book of matches out of her pocket and lit one of the matches.

"Kids, don't try this at home," she said. "I'm a professional."

Then she blew out the match. Smoke started rising up from it. Mrs. Meyer held the match under the smoke detector.

Beep! Beep! Beep! Beep! went the smoke detector.

"It looks like your smoke detector works perfectly," said Mrs. Meyer. "Isn't that an annoying sound?"

"Yes," said Mr. Cooper. "I hate that sound."

"Me too," said everybody, because *every-body* hates that beeping sound that smoke detectors make.

Beep! Beep! Beep! Beep!

"Can you please turn it off now?" asked Andrea. "That noise hurts my ears."

"One second," said Mrs. Meyer as she fiddled with the smoke detector.

Beep! Beep! Beep! Beep!

For once I had to agree with Andrea. That beeping is the most annoying sound in the history of the world.

Beep! Beep! Beep! Beep!

"Maybe you should take out the battery," suggested Mr. Cooper.

"I'm *trying* to take out the battery," said Mrs. Meyer. "The little battery door on the

30

smoke detector is stuck."

Beep! Beep! Beep! Beep!

It was horrible! I thought I was gonna die. We were all holding our hands over our ears to keep out the noise. Mrs. Meyer was having trouble taking the battery out of the smoke detector.

Beep! Beep! Beep! Beep!

"My head is gonna explode!" I shouted.

Beep! Beep! Beep! Beep!

"It's driving me crazy!" shouted Emily. "We've got to *do* something!"

Beep! Beep! Beep! Beep!

"Quick, get me the fire extinguisher," hollered Mrs. Meyer.

Mr. Cooper grabbed the fire extinguisher and handed it to her.

"Are you going to shoot the fire extinguisher at the smoke detector to turn it off?" asked Andrea.

"Not exactly," said Mrs. Meyer.

That's when the most amazing thing in the history of the world happened. Mrs. Meyer put the smoke detector on the floor. Then she raised the fire extinguisher over her head and smashed it down on top of the smoke detector!

Smash! Crack!

"Oh, snap!" said Ryan. "She totally crushed it!"

Ryan was right. Mrs. Meyer had broken the smoke detector into pieces. That thing wouldn't be detecting any smoke for a long time.

BEEP BEEP BEEP

Busting stuff up is cool. They should have a TV channel where they just bust stuff up all day long. I would watch that channel every day.

But that's when something even *more* amazing happened.

Beep! Beep! Beep! Beep!

The smoke detector was still beeping even though it was busted into pieces! Nobody could believe it!

Mrs. Meyer picked up the fire extinguisher again and slammed it down on one of the pieces of the smoke detector. *Smash!*

Beep! Beep! Beep! Beep!

It was *still* beeping! Mrs. Meyer looked

really mad. She picked up the fire extinguisher and slammed it down on the
smoke detector over and over again. She
looked like a crazy person! It was like that
horror movie I saw once, *The Thing That
Wouldn't Die.*

"I'm not sure I approve of this violence,"
said Andrea. "It sets a bad example for
children."

"What do you have against violins?" I
asked Andrea.

"Not violins, Arlo! Violence!"

Finally, Mrs. Meyer stopped hitting the
smoke detector. She was sweating and
shaking and panting. There were little
pieces of smoke detector all over the floor.

I thought one of them might start beeping again, but everything was quiet.

"Well, thank you for that informative
lesson about fire safety," said Mr. Cooper.

"And I think we all learned a new use for fire extinguishers."

Mrs. Meyer wiped off her face and said she had to go talk to the other classes.

"One more thing," she said when she reached the door. "It's time to replace your smoke detector. This one is broken."

And then she left.

Mrs. Meyer is weird.

Stop, Drop, and Roll!

We were sitting in Mr. Cooper's class the next day. He told us to turn to page twenty-three in our math books. And you'll never believe in a million hundred years what happened at that moment.

Lights started flashing! Sirens started screaming! And Mrs. Meyer came into the room.

Mr. Cooper rolled his eyes. He put his math book down.

"To what do we owe the pleasure of your company *today*, Mrs. Meyer?" he asked.

"I have a joke for you," said Mrs. Meyer.

Oh no, not another joke!

"What did the firefighter name her twin sons?" she asked.

"I give up," said Ryan.

"I give up," said Michael.

"I give up," said Alexia.

In case you were wondering, everybody was saying they give up.

"She named her first son José," said Mrs. Meyer, "and she named her second son Hose B! Get it?"

I didn't get it. Why would somebody

name their son after a hose? Mrs. Meyer's jokes are terrible. But I pretended to laugh anyway because everybody else was laughing.

"Yesterday we talked about preventing fires," said Mrs. Meyer. "Today I'd like to talk about what you should do if there *is* a fire in your house."

Mrs. Meyer had lots of good advice. She told us that before opening a door, we should touch the doorknob and put our hand on the crack around the door. If you feel heat, there may be fire on the other side of the door. She also told us that if your room is on fire, you should stay low to the floor because smoke rises. The air you can breathe will be near the floor. She sure knew a lot about fire.

"Now, let's say your clothes catch on fire, and you don't have a fire extinguisher," said Mrs. Meyer. "What should you do?"

Andrea was saying *"Oooooh oooooh ooooh"* and waving her hand around like she was cleaning a big window with a rag. But Mrs. Meyer called on me instead. So nah-nah-nah boo-boo on Andrea.

"If your clothes catch on fire," I said, "you should get new clothes."

Everybody laughed even though I didn't say anything funny.

"Uh, no," said Mrs. Meyer.

Hmmm. I decided to guess again.

"If your clothes catch on fire, you should run," I said.

"Actually, that's the *worst* thing to do," said Mrs. Meyer. "Running will fan the flames and make things worse."

Andrea smiled the smile she smiles whenever I get something wrong. Then she stuck her tongue out at me. Why can't a truck full of flaming clothes fall on her head?

"If your clothes catch on fire," Mrs. Meyer told us, "stop what you're doing. Drop to the ground. Cover your face with your hands. And roll over and over again until the flames are out."

"That makes sense," said Mr. Cooper.

"Stop, drop, and roll!" shouted Mrs. Meyer. "Repeat after me. Stop, drop, and roll!"

"Stop, drop, and roll!" we all chanted. "Stop, drop, and roll!"

"That's right!" said Mrs. Meyer. "And let's say your bedroom is on fire, and there's smoke everywhere. What do you do?"

"Hide in your closet!" I shouted.

"Actually, that's the worst place to go," said Mrs. Meyer.

Andrea stuck her tongue out at me again.

"If your bedroom is on fire," said Mrs. Meyer, "fall and crawl! Repeat after me. Fall and crawl!"

"Fall and crawl!" we all chanted. "Fall and crawl!"

"If there's a fire in your house, don't hide. Go outside!" said Mrs. Meyer. "Repeat after me. Don't hide. Go outside!"

"Don't hide. Go outside!" we all chanted. "Don't hide. Go outside!"

Sheesh, Mrs. Meyer must *really* like chanting.

"Okay, now let's pretend there's a fire right here in this classroom," said Mrs. Meyer. "You touched the door. It's really hot. You need to find another way out. What are you going to do?"

"Stop, drop, and roll!" shouted Neil the

nude kid. "Stop, drop, and roll!"

"Fall and crawl!" shouted Emily.

"Don't hide. Go outside!" shouted Alexia.

"That's right!" said Mrs. Meyer. "Go outside. Follow me, kids!"

And you'll never guess in a million hundred years what happened next.

I'm not going to tell you.

Okay, okay, I'll tell you.

Mrs. Meyer jumped out the window!

That's right! She jumped right out the window! We saw it with our own eyes!

Well, duh, it would be hard to see it with somebody else's eyes.

Mrs. Meyer sure is lucky that our classroom is on the first floor of the school. If it was on the third floor, jumping out the window would have been a really dumb move.

We were all too shocked to do anything. Mrs. Meyer was standing on the grass outside our classroom, waving for us to follow her.

"I'm not jumping out the window," said Andrea.

"Me neither," said Emily, who always agrees with everything Andrea says.

"Let's go!" shouted Mrs. Meyer. "Your classroom is on fire! There's smoke everywhere! What are you waiting for? Don't hide. Go outside!"

Then she started blowing a whistle.

I looked at Michael. Michael looked at Ryan. Ryan looked at Neil. Neil looked at Alexia. Alexia looked at Mr. Cooper.

That's when the most amazing thing in the history of the world happened.

Mr. Cooper jumped out the window!

"Hurry up!" Mr. Cooper shouted at us. "The building is going up in flames! Quick, before it's too late!"

"Go! Go! Go!" shouted Mrs. Meyer, blowing her whistle over and over.

So we all jumped out the window. Even Andrea and Emily. It was cool.

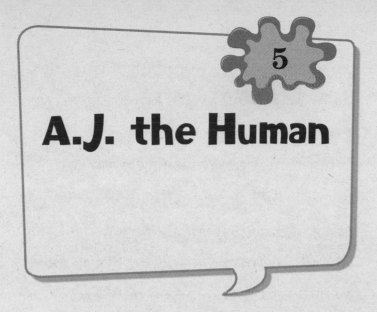

A.J. the Human

We were sitting in class the next day, minding our own business. Mr. Cooper told us to open our math books. But then, suddenly, lights started flashing. Sirens started screaming. And you'll never believe who ran into the door at that moment.

Nobody! Why would you run into a door? That would hurt. I thought we went over that in chapter 3.

But you'll never believe who ran into the door*way*.

No, it *wasn't* Mrs. Meyer. Ha! You thought it was Mrs. Meyer. But it wasn't. So nah-nah-nah boo-boo on you.

Actually, it wasn't a person who ran into the doorway. It was a *bear*! And the bear was wearing a hat and holding a shovel!

Everybody started yelling and screaming and shrieking and hooting and hollering and hiding under their desks and generally freaking out.

"Eeeeeeek!" went all the girls.

"There's a bear in the class!" shouted Ryan.

"Help!" shouted Neil. "Run for your lives!"

Actually, this wasn't the first time a bear came into our school. One time my job was to be the door closer, but I forgot to close the door and a bear walked right into the gym! You should have been there!*

The point is, bears come into our school pretty frequently.

"Eeeeeeek!"

"Stop!" shouted the bear, holding its hand up. "Wait! Calm down!"

That was weird. Since when do bears talk? And since when do bears wear hats and carry shovels?

---

*If you weren't, you can read about it in a book called *Mr. Jack Is a Maniac!*

"Something tells me that is not a real bear," said Mr. Cooper.

"I think it might be Mrs. Meyer in a bear costume," said Ryan. "It sounds just like her."

"Are you Mrs. Meyer?" Andrea asked the bear.

"Meyer?" said the bear. "Never heard of her. My name is Woodsy the Bear."

Woodsy the Bear? That's a weird name. It was *obvious* that Woodsy was a bear. He didn't need to have the last name Bear. That would be like me calling myself A.J. the Human.

"I'm here to teach you how to prevent forest fires," said Woodsy the Bear.

Everybody calmed down. Woodsy said we should always build our campfires fifteen feet away from tents, shrubs, trees, or branches that could catch on fire. Then he said to get rid of grass, twigs, and leaves in the area. He told us to circle the fire pit with rocks and to keep a bucket of water and a shovel nearby in case of emergency. Woodsy gave us lots of good advice about making a campfire in the woods. Then he told us that he had to go talk to the other classes.

"Wow, you sure know a lot about preventing forest fires," I told Woodsy. "You probably know as much as Mrs. Meyer."

"Remember," Woodsy told me, "only *you*

can prevent forest fires."

Only me? Wow, that's a lot of pressure. I started getting nervous.

"What about Ryan?" I asked. "Can't he prevent forest fires?"

"Well, yes, Ryan too," said Woodsy the Bear. "I really must go visit the other classes now."

"How about Neil?" I asked. "Can Neil prevent forest fires?"

"Uh, yeah," said Woodsy the Bear. "I suppose Neil can also prevent forest fires. Look, I'm sorry, but I must go."

"And Michael?" I asked. "Can *he* prevent forest fires?"

"Yeah. Sure. Anybody can," said Woodsy impatiently.

"Then why didn't you say so?" I asked.

"It's just an expression," said Woodsy the Bear. "When I said only you can prevent forest fires, I meant everybody can prevent forest fires."

That made no sense at all. If he meant everybody can prevent forest fires, he should have said that in the first place. It was like when Mrs. Meyer told us we should put smoke detectors on the floor when she really meant we should put them on the ceiling. People should say what they mean.

"What about aliens from other planets?" I asked. "Can *they* prevent forest fires?"

"I'm outta here," Woodsy the Bear said.

Then he turned and left.

Woodsy the Bear is weird.

You're Welcome!

You know how your parents and teachers say you have to read a chapter of a book every night? Sometimes you just don't want to, because reading books is hard. And then your mom or dad yells and screams and nags you about it, right? I know what it's like. My parents do that to me all the time.

Don't you wish there was a *really* short chapter you could knock off in five minutes so you could go do fun stuff like play video games or watch TV?

Well, your old pal A.J. has the solution to your problem.

And this is it! Chapter 6. That's right—  you just read it. It's over. Done. Now you can tell your parents that you finished a chapter in a book today. So nah-nah-nah boo-boo on them.

You're welcome!

Drill, Baby, Drill

Every day, Mr. Cooper tries to teach us how to do math. I don't know why. What's the point of learning math when we have calculators?

Anyway, Mr. Cooper had just told us to turn to page twenty-three in our math books when lights started flashing and sirens started screaming. And you'll never believe in a million hundred years what happened next.

No, Mrs. Meyer *didn't* come running into the doorway. Wrong again!

"Fire drill!" everybody started shouting.

Yay! A fire drill is when we have to pretend there's a fire even though nothing is burning up. It's kind of like having an imaginary friend who you talk to but isn't really there. I used to have an imaginary friend named Johnny, but we got into an argument, and now we're not speaking to each other anymore.

Fire drills are cool because we get to miss math and reading and other boring stuff. If you ask me, we should have a fire drill every day.

We had to get up and walk single file out of the building. Mr. Cooper was the line leader. Alexia was the door holder. Everybody was goofing around, because we knew it wasn't a real fire. If it was a real fire, I would have run out of there like a cheetah was chasing me.

"Walk quickly, kids!" Mr. Cooper told us. "No talking."

We had to stand out on the playground for a million hundred hours because I guess that's how long it takes a school to burn down.

So we were standing out there minding our own business, and you'll never believe what I saw coming out of the trees next to the playground.

Smoke.

"Hey, look over there!" I said, pointing toward the woods.

"It looks like a forest fire might be starting!" yelled Andrea.

"Oh no!" hollered Michael.

"Run for your lives!" shouted Neil.

"We've got to *do* something!" hollered Emily.

"That's right," yelled Ryan. "Only all of us can prevent forest fires!"

"Let's go!" said Mr. Cooper as he pulled out his cell phone. "I'll call the school and tell them to alert the fire department."

We ran into the woods to see if we could put out the forest fire. And you'll never believe in a million hundred years what we found there.

It was Mrs. Meyer!

She was sitting next to a little campfire, holding a long stick with a hot dog at the end of it.

"What are you doing here, Mrs. Meyer?" asked Michael.

"What does it *look* like I'm doing?" she replied. "I'm cooking a hot dog. I never got to eat breakfast today."

"Did you make that fire with your own hands?" asked Alexia.

"Well, I couldn't make it with somebody else's hands," she said, taking a bite of her hot dog. "Did any of you kids ever make a campfire?"

"No," said Neil.

"No," said Andrea.

"No," said Emily.

In case you were wondering, everybody was saying no.

"There are three things you need to make a fire," Mrs. Meyer told us as she took another bite of her hot dog. "Can anybody name one of them?"

"Lighter fluid!" I shouted.

"You're partly right, A.J.," she said. "You need fuel, air, and heat. The fuel is needed for the fire to burn. The air is needed for the fire to breathe. And the heat is needed to keep the fire burning. If you get rid of any one of those three things, your fire will go out."

Boy, she sure knew a lot about making a fire. She should get the Nobel Prize. That's a prize they give out to people who know how to make fires. Mrs. Meyer took the last bite of her hot dog.

"If fire is so dangerous, why would we want to make one?" asked Andrea.

"So you can toast marshmallows, silly!" said Mrs. Meyer.

Marshmallows! I *love* marshmallows. I can't think of anything in the world I love more than marshmallows.

Well, maybe chocolate. And ice cream. And pizza.

But I really like marshmallows, too. Mrs. Meyer pulled out a big bag of them and gave each of us a pointy stick. She showed us how to hold the marshmallow over the fire and turn it really slowly so it gets browned on all sides.

"Toasty brown all around!" Mrs. Meyer said. "Repeat after me. Toasty brown all around!"

"Toasty brown all around!" we all chanted.

I ate about a million hundred marshmallows. I thought I was gonna throw up.
It was the greatest day of my life.

"Say, do you kids want to hear a joke?"
Mrs. Meyer asked as we were toasting our
marshmallows.

Oh no. Not again. Mrs. Meyer's jokes are awful.

"Did you hear about the fire at the circus?" she asked us.

"No," we all replied.

"It was in tents," said Mrs. Meyer.

That was the whole joke. I didn't get it. Of *course* it was in tents. It was at the circus! Mrs. Meyer's jokes make no sense at all.

After we finished all the marshmallows, Mrs. Meyer just sat there, staring into the fire without saying anything for a long time. She looked all glassy-eyed. It was like she was in a trance or something.

"Fire is an amazing thing, don't you think?" she finally said. "It can be so useful, and also so destructive."

Like I said, Mrs. Meyer is weird.*

---

*Are you enjoying the story so far? Good. So what are you reading this for? The story's up there, dumbhead!

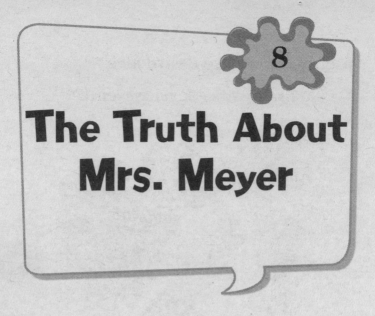

The Truth About Mrs. Meyer

We were eating lunch in the vomitorium. I had a peanut butter and jelly sandwich. Michael had a peanut butter and jelly sandwich. Ryan had a peanut butter and jelly sandwich. *Everybody* had peanut butter and jelly sandwiches. I traded my peanut butter and jelly sandwich for Neil's peanut butter and jelly sandwich because his mom cuts the crusts off.

"You know what's weird?" I told the gang. "Sometimes they say that a house burned down. And sometimes they say that a house burned up. But it's the same thing!"

"That's right," said Ryan. "Whether your house burns up or down, you still have no house left."

"I'll tell you what's weird," said Michael. "Mrs. Meyer."

"Yeah!" we all agreed.

"She's always telling jokes about fire," said Alexia.

"Hey, I know a fire joke," I said. "What

do you call a doll that's on fire?"

"What?" everybody asked.

"A Barbie-Q."

Everybody laughed. Neil the nude kid laughed so hard that milk came out of his nose. You know a joke is good if you can make milk come out of somebody's nose. That's the first rule of being a kid.

I didn't see it, but annoying Andrea and crybaby Emily had just come up behind us. They put their trays on our table.

"Setting dolls on fire is *not* funny, Arlo," said Andrea. "How would you like it if I set one of your action figures on fire?"

"I did that last week," I told her. "His face melted off. It was cool."

Andrea and Emily sat down. Andrea had on her mean face, as usual.

"What's eating you?" I asked her. "Did they cancel your clog-dancing lesson for today?"*

"No," Andrea said. "I'm worried about Mrs. Meyer. I think she likes fire a little *too* much."

---

*That's a kind of dance that plumbers do.

"Yeah, did you see the look in her eyes when she was staring into the campfire?" asked Alexia. "It was creepy. I think Mrs. Meyer is obsessed with fire."

"Maybe she's a pyromaniac," said Andrea.

"You mean she really loves eating pie?" I asked.

Everybody laughed even though I didn't say anything funny.

"No, dumbhead," said Andrea. "A pyromaniac is somebody who can't stop setting fires."

"I knew that," I lied. "Hey, maybe Mrs. Meyer isn't a real firefighter at *all*. Maybe she's an imposter."

"Stop trying to scare Emily," Andrea told me.

"Yeah, maybe Mrs. Meyer is a pyro-maniac who is just *pretending* to be a firefighter," said Michael.

"I'm scared," said Emily.

"Maybe Mrs. Meyer kidnapped a real firefighter and tied him up in an abandoned barn," said Neil. "Stuff like that happens all the time, you know."

"And she's about to set the barn on fire!" said Ryan. "I saw that in a movie once."

"She'll probably set our school on fire," I added.

"We've got to *do* something!" Emily shouted. And then she went running out of the room.

Sheesh. That girl will fall for *anything*.

Mrs. Meyer Is a Liar

Actually, Emily was right. We *did* have to do something. If Mrs. Meyer was going to set the school on fire, a lot of people could get hurt.

There was only one thing for us to do. We had to go talk to Mr. Klutz.

After lunch the whole gang and I

skipped recess and went to Mr. Klutz's office instead.

Well, we didn't just go to his office. We snuck down the hallways, ducking into doorways along the way so Mrs. Meyer wouldn't see us. It was exciting! There was electricity in the air.

Well, not really. If there was electricity in the air, we would have all been

electrocuted. And that's even worse than catching on *fire*. But we were slinking around like secret agents. It was cool.

Mr. Klutz was standing in front of his office talking to some parent.

"Blah blah my daughter blah blah," said the parent. "Blah blah she won't do it again blah blah."

"Blah blah thank you blah blah," said Mr. Klutz. "Blah blah we appreciate your blah blah."

Grown-ups are really boring. After a million hundred minutes, the parent finally said good-bye to Mr. Klutz and left.

"What can I do for you kids?" Mr. Klutz asked us. "Aren't you missing recess?"

"We have an important question we need to ask you," said Andrea. "Is Mrs. Meyer a *real* firefighter?"

"Hmmm," said Mr. Klutz, scratching his head as if he had any hair up there.

"We're afraid she's a pyromaniac who kidnapped a *real* firefighter," I told him. "She probably tied him up in an abandoned barn, and she's about to set it on fire."

"Hmmm," said Mr. Klutz, scratching his head again. He must have had a rash or something. "Mrs. Meyer *told* me she's a real firefighter. She *looks* like a real firefighter. She *talks* like a real firefighter. But I can't be completely sure. Maybe you

should ask her to prove that she's a real firefighter."

"Yeah!" Alexia said. "Let's make her prove it."

"Yeah!" we all agreed.

"Where *is* Mrs. Meyer?" asked Andrea.

"Oh, she's not here," said Mr. Klutz. "She said she wanted to take the rest of the day off, but the fire chief told her she had to go to the firehouse for an important meeting at three fifteen."

"Important meeting?" I said. "Ha! Mrs. Meyer is a liar. I bet she didn't even go to the firehouse, because she's not a real firefighter. She's a fake!"

That's when I got the greatest idea in the history of the world.

I looked at Ryan. Ryan looked at Neil. Neil looked at Andrea. Andrea looked at Alexia. We were all looking at each other, because we all had the same genius idea.

Important meeting? Three fifteen? We get out of school at three o'clock.

We were going to spy on Mrs. Meyer.

A Real Spy
Mission

As soon as the three-o'clock bell rang, we all ran out of school and gathered in the playground. This was going to be a real spy mission.

"Okay, let's synchronize our watches," I said, because that's what they always do in spy movies.

"I don't have a watch," said Ryan.

"Me neither," said Neil.

Actually, I didn't have a watch either. It just sounds cool to say "Let's synchronize our watches."

"I have a watch," said Andrea. "It's five minutes after three."

Of *course* Andrea had a watch. She's probably the only third grader in the world who wears a watch.

"Okay," I said. "The big meeting at the firehouse starts in ten minutes. Let's go!"

The firehouse is just three blocks from school. We slinked down the street like secret agents, ducking into doorways and hiding behind mailboxes along the way so nobody would see us. It was cool.

Finally, we reached the firehouse. There was a giant garage door where the fire trucks drive in and out.

"I'm scared," said Emily as we lurked next to the door.

"If Mrs. Meyer isn't in there," whispered Alexia, "that's proof that she isn't a real firefighter."

"And if there's no meeting going on in here," whispered Michael, "that means Mrs. Meyer is a liar."

"Shhhhhh!" whispered Andrea, looking at her watch. "It's three fifteen right *now*."

We peeked our heads around the wall so we could snoop on what was happening

inside the fire-house.

"Do you see anything?" Neil whispered.

"No," whispered Michael. "There's nobody in there. The place is empty."

"Nothing's going on," whispered Ryan. "There's no meeting."

"That's proof!" I whispered. "See? I *told* you Mrs. Meyer wasn't a real firefighter. She's probably home watching TV and eating bonbons."

"Shhhhhhh!" whispered Andrea.

That's when the most amazing thing in the history of the world happened.

Mrs. Meyer came walking down the street.

Well, that's not the amazing part, because Mrs. Meyer probably walks down the street all the time. The amazing part was what happened next.

Mrs. Meyer was coming from the other direction. She didn't see us.

"Look!" whispered Emily. "She's going into the firehouse!"

At that moment lights started flashing. Sirens started screaming. Bells started ringing. Whistles started blowing. Alarms started sounding. My ears started hurting.

"It must be a fire!" shouted Ryan. "We gotta get outta here!"

But it *wasn't* a fire. If it was a fire, all the firefighters would have jumped on the fire truck and driven out of the firehouse. Instead, they all jumped out from *behind* the fire truck and yelled at Mrs. Meyer . . .

"SURPRISE!"

A giant banner came down from the ceiling. . . .

"It's not a fire," said Michael. "It's Mrs. Meyer's birthday!"

"They're throwing her a surprise party!"
said Andrea. "That's so sweet!"

Andrea was right for once in her life.
All the firefighters gathered around Mrs.

Meyer. They were hugging her and giving her presents.

"So I guess she really *is* a firefighter after all," said Alexia.

Well, we had accomplished our spy mission. We were about to turn around and go home. But that's when the most amazing thing in the history of the world happened.

"What are you kids doing here?" Mrs. Meyer suddenly asked.

She had spotted us! I didn't know what to say. I didn't know what to do. I had to think fast.

"We ... uh ... came to wish you a happy birthday," I said.

"Great!" said Mrs. Meyer. "You're just in time for the party!"

Mrs. Meyer took us inside the firehouse and introduced us to all the other firefighters. They let us climb on a fire truck, which was really cool. And we got to pet their fire dog. But the coolest part was when they took us up to the second floor and let us slide down the fire poles. That was so much more fun than taking the stairs. I'm going to get my parents to put a fire pole in our house.

Emily was too scared, but the rest of us slid down the fire poles a million hundred times. Then one of the firefighters wheeled in a giant cake.

Cake! I love cake!

"This will make up for the cake I didn't get to eat on *my* birthday," said Emily.

Mrs. Meyer must be really old, because that cake had a *lot* of candles on it. Two of the firefighters lit them, and then we all sang "Happy Birthday."

"Make a wish," one of the firefighters told Mrs. Meyer.

She closed her eyes. That's when the weirdest thing in the history of the world happened.

But I'm not going to tell you what it was.

Okay, okay, I'll tell you. But you have to read the next chapter. So nah-nah-nah boo-boo on you!

11

Mrs. Meyer Gets Fired

Mrs. Meyer had her eyes closed, so she didn't see what happened next. But I did. The banner that said HAPPY BIRTHDAY MRS. MEYER had been tied to the fire pole on the second floor. I guess it wasn't tied very tightly, because it slowly started to slide down.

It was coming down right over the cake!
The banner touched the candles on the cake!
The candles lit the banner on fire!

"Eeeeeeek!" went all the girls.

"It's on fire!" Ryan shouted.

"Call the fire department!" I shouted.

"This *is* the fire department!" shouted Andrea.

"Then call the police department!" I shouted.

The banner was burning up. Everybody started yelling and screaming and shrieking and hooting and hollering and generally freaking out.*

"Help!" shouted Neil. "Run for your lives!"

"Get the hose!" shouted one of the firefighters.

---

*Want to laugh your head off? Ask a parent if you can go on YouTube. Then search for "Fire Marshall Bill" and watch the videos with Jim Carrey. They are hilarious.

"The hose is on fire!" shouted another firefighter.

"The firehouse is on fire!" I shouted.

The banner was going up in flames, and some of the letters had burned up. Instead of reading HAPPY BIRTHDAY MRS. MEYER, all that was left was HA IR D YE!

"Get a fire extinguisher!" somebody yelled. "Mrs. Meyer is on fire!"

It was true. Part of the banner had landed on Mrs. Meyer's pants, and now *they* were on fire.

"Stop, drop, and roll!" shouted Andrea.

"Fall and crawl!" shouted Alexia.

"Get low and go!" shouted Ryan.

"Don't hide. Go outside!" shouted Neil.

"Toasty brown all around!" I shouted.

The firefighters squirted that foamy stuff all over Mrs. Meyer until they put her out. The only problem was that now the *cake* was on fire.

"The cake is on fire!" somebody shouted. "Shoot the cake!"

It was true! Flames were coming out of the frosting! What's up with *that*? Whoever heard of a cake that caught on fire? That cake must have been made with gasoline or something.

There were sirens screaming and lights flashing. Smoke was everywhere. The firefighters were shooting fire extinguishers and hoses all over the place. Everybody was slipping on goopy cake and falling all over the floor. What a mess! It was hilarious. And we got to see it live and in person.

Finally, after a million hundred minutes, the firefighters put the fires out. We all wished Mrs. Meycr a happy birthday and left the firehouse.

In the end we didn't get to eat any cake. *Again*. Man, I hate birthdays. Especially birthdays when you don't get any cake. Bummer in the summer!

Well, that's pretty much what happened. Maybe next year crybaby Emily will get to eat some birthday cake. Maybe they'll put trampolines in our class instead of desks. Maybe Mr. Cooper will use his super vision to shoot microwave-freezing rays out of his eyes. Maybe we'll eat Mr. Klutz's melon head. Maybe I'll get to pee on another campfire. Maybe Mrs. Meyer will stop telling bad jokes, destroying smoke detectors, and jumping out of windows. Maybe they'll start a TV channel where they just bust stuff up all day long.

Maybe firefighters will stop naming their children after hoses. Maybe my mom will start cutting the crusts off my peanut butter and jelly sandwiches. Maybe bears will stop running into our school. Maybe I'll melt the face off another one of my action figures. Maybe they'll make smoke detectors in the shape of a nose. Maybe I can talk my parents into putting a fire pole in our house.

But it won't be easy!